Travel Adventures

YELLOWSTONE

Volume

Ben Nussbaum

Consultants

Lisa Ellick, M.A.
Math Specialist
Norfolk Public Schools

Pamela Estrada, M.S.Ed.
Teacher
Westminster School District

Publishing Credits

Rachelle Cracchiolo, M.S.Ed., *Publisher*
Conni Medina, M.A.Ed., *Managing Editor*
Dona Herweck Rice, *Series Developer*
Emily R. Smith, M.A.Ed., *Series Developer*
Diana Kenney, M.A.Ed., NBCT, *Content Director*
Stacy Monsman, M.A., *Editor*
Kristy Stark, M.A.Ed., *Editor*
Kevin Panter, *Graphic Designer*

Image Credits: p.7 Dennis Kunkel Microscopy/Science Source; pp.14 (top), 24 (top) Jim Peaco, courtesy of Yellowstone National Park; p.24 (bottom) Norbert Rosing/Getty Images; p.26 F. J. Haynes, courtesy National Park Service; all other images from iStock and/or Shutterstock.

Library of Congress Cataloging-in-Publication Data

Names: Nussbaum, Ben, 1975- author.
Title: Travel adventures: Yellowstone / Ben Nussbaum.
Other titles: Yellowstone
Description: Huntington Beach, CA : Teacher Created Materials, 2018. | Includes index. | Audience: Grade 4 to 6.
Identifiers: LCCN 2017033187 (print) | LCCN 2017034228 (ebook) | ISBN 9781425859558 (eBook) | ISBN 9781425858094 (pbk.)
Subjects: LCSH: Yellowstone National Park--Juvenile literature.
Classification: LCC F722 (ebook) | LCC F722 .N94 2018 (print) | DDC 978.7/52--dc23
LC record available at https://lccn.loc.gov/2017033187

Teacher Created Materials
5301 Oceanus Drive
Huntington Beach, CA 92649-1030
http://www.tcmpub.com

ISBN 978-1-4258-5809-4

Made in China
Nordica.112017.CA21701237

Table of Contents

An Enchanted Land

There's a place in America that is still wild. Bears, wolves, and cougars live free. Bison graze in mountain meadows. Moose and elk do, too. Eagles and falcons soar in the sky. It's a land of waterfalls and snow-covered peaks. Yellowstone National Park is filled with many beautiful sights. But, Yellowstone is also a bizarre and dangerous place. Underground heat melts roads. The ground shakes with earthquakes. Geysers shoot into the air. Yellowstone is full of **contradictions**. It's wild, but it is also carefully under control. It's peaceful, but that peace can be shattered at any minute.

American Indians lived there first. It wasn't long until white settlers found the land. One of the first non-Indians to see Yellowstone was a **prospector** named John C. Davis. In 1864, he wrote that his group was stunned by "the wonders of this **enchanted** land." He added, "We hardly knew what to think."

Today, millions of people visit Yellowstone each year. People come from all over the world to see the wonders that Davis wrote about.

Bison graze by a river.

A geyser shoots water and steam into the air at Yellowstone National Park.

LET'S EXPLORE MATH

Visitors to Yellowstone often use horses, mules, or llamas to carry their gear. These animals can carry pack boxes on their backs.

Suppose a pack box in the shape of a rectangular prism has a length of 30 inches, width of 15 inches, and height of 20 inches. Which of the following best describes the volume of the pack box? Describe your reasoning.

- **A.** 9,000
- **B.** 9,000 inches
- **C.** 9,000 square inches
- **D.** 9,000 cubic inches

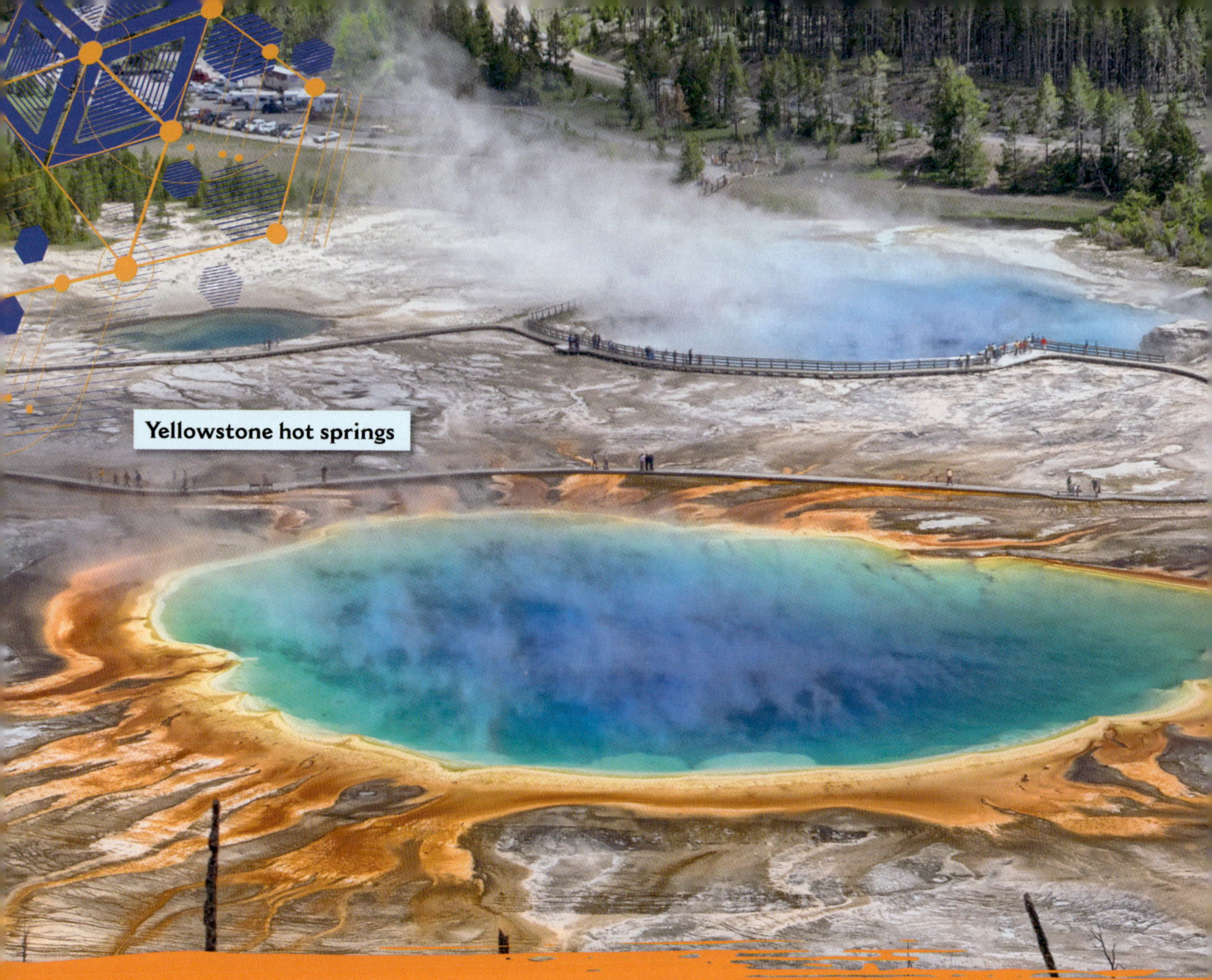

Yellowstone hot springs

A Real Hot Spot

A volcano isn't visible when tourists visit Yellowstone. That's because *all* of Yellowstone is a supervolcano, right underfoot. It gurgles and burps. It gently shakes the ground.

The park is located on a **plateau** about 8,000 feet (2,438 meters) above sea level. **Magma** pushes through cracks in the volcano. When rainwater falls in Yellowstone, it seeps through the surface and meets the heat beneath. Hot springs are created when this hot water flows back up to the surface.

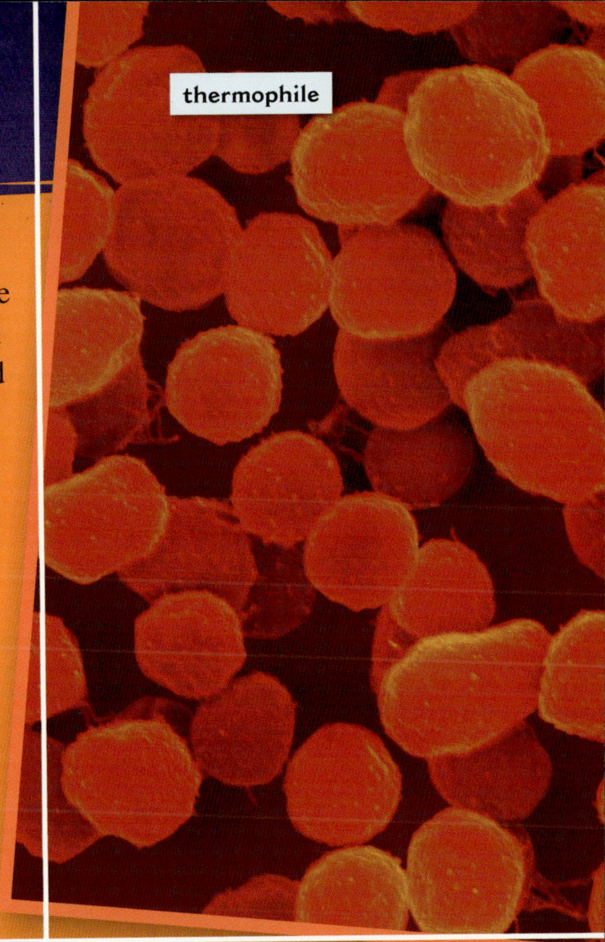

The water slowly cools toward the edge of the hot spring. Tiny **organisms** live in this unique environment. They are called **thermophiles**. That means "heat lovers" in Greek.

Different thermophiles prefer different water temperatures. The colored rings of a hot spring indicate the type of thermophiles that live in that water. Park visitors marvel at the beautiful colors that result.

The Grand Prismatic Spring is one of these hot springs. It's Yellowstone's largest. It's as long as two football fields and over 100 ft. (30 m) deep.

LET'S EXPLORE MATH

Thermophiles can form layers which appear solid. These are called *mats*. Suppose scientists take a sample from a mat to study. They draw the sample to record its size. Each cubic unit stands for 1 cubic centimeter. Use the drawing to answer the questions.

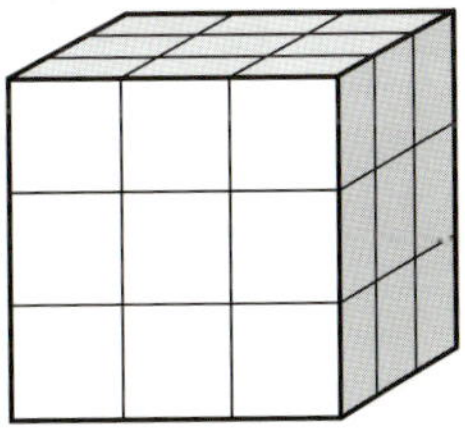

1. How many layers are in the sample?
2. How many cubic centimeters are in one layer?
3. How many cubic centimeters are in the sample?

A rainbow forms over Old Faithful.

Geysers are a type of hot spring. They form when water is heated underground. However, that water can't make it to the surface. The water becomes very hot. As the temperature increases, so does the pressure. When the pressure is too great, water bursts through the surface and into the sky.

Yellowstone has more than 300 geysers. That is more than half of the world's total geysers! Old Faithful is one of the park's most famous geysers. It erupts about 17 times each day. It can shoot water as high as 180 ft. (55 m). Steamboat is a geyser that does not erupt on a predictable schedule. But, when it does, it can blast water 300 ft. (91 m) into the sky. Castle shoots water out of a large cone. Some people think it looks like the ruins of an ancient fortress. Its blasts can last 20 minutes and are followed by 30 to 40 minutes of steam. Comet has a very small eruption, but it erupts almost constantly. All of these geysers can create rainbows on sunny days when light passes through their mist.

Amazing Animals

Yellowstone is home to lots of animals, such as bison, black bears, and wolves. In fact, there are 67 types of mammals in the park! Yellowstone has the largest concentration of mammals in the continental United States.

Lynx, bobcats, and cougars are some of the fierce **predators** that live there. Many of them have made Yellowstone their home because there is a lot of small prey to eat. These giant cats compete with wolves and bears for food, but they are rarely seen by visitors.

Mammals aren't the park's only creatures. Cutthroat trout and other fish fill Yellowstone's streams. Lizards warm themselves in the sun. Frogs croak the days away in the ponds.

About 150 species of birds nest in the park. The trumpeter swan was almost **extinct** a generation ago. The park gave it a safe home. Now, the species is rebounding. Bald eagles nest near water. Ospreys (AH-sprays) dive to catch fish.

bobcat

Many of Yellowstone's creatures move in and out of the park. Luckily, much of the wilderness around Yellowstone is also protected. The park and the surrounding areas are known as the Greater Yellowstone **Ecosystem**.

trumpeter swan

American bald eagle
grizzly bear

Bison

Yellowstone is home to about 5,000 bison. Park visitors often see them. The large beasts spend a lot of time in open meadows where they can find grass to eat. In some places, roads run right next to where they graze. Groups of bison often block traffic. They are not afraid of humans.

Bison may seem tame, but people must remember that they are wild animals. Bison are not normally **aggressive**, but they will protect themselves. Some bison have attacked people who try to take photos with them. This is not something to take lightly. Male bison can weigh about 2,000 pounds (907 kilograms). They can run faster than an **elite** sprinter. They can even jump up to 6 ft. (2 m) in the air. It's best to always give wild animals some space.

In the late 1800s, bison were almost extinct. The herd in the park helped the species survive. Now, the park often has too many bison. Each year, some of the animals are given to American Indian tribes whose ancestors once hunted bison. The people use the bison meat and hides for food, clothing, and other needs.

a bison and her calf

herd of bison

LET'S EXPLORE MATH

If bison seem sick, rangers put them in pens as a form of quarantine. They feed the bison hay.

Imagine that the hay bale is in the shape of a rectangular prism. Each cubic unit in the drawing stands for 1 cubic meter. Use the drawing to complete the sentence frames.

There are ______ layers of ______ cubic meters. The hay bale has a volume of ______ cubic meters.

A bear explores a park dumpster.

A grizzly bear and her three cubs walk through the park in search of food.

Bears

Imagine driving through Yellowstone. You see a bear by the side of the road. Your parent stops the car to get a closer look. Before you can blink, the bear sticks its nose through your car window. The bear is looking for your picnic lunch.

It's hard to believe, but interactions between humans and bears used to be common. Many bears and people were injured as a result of this close **proximity**.

Times have changed. Park rangers do not want bears to develop a taste for human food, so people are not allowed to feed them. The park has strict rules to keep people and bears from getting too close to each other. Trash is locked away so bears can't see it. People must also stay at least 100 yards (91 meters) away from bears.

The park is home to black bears and grizzly bears. Black bears weigh about as much as a grown man. Grizzly bears are bigger. They weigh up to 700 lb. (318 kg)! In 1975, about 130 grizzlies lived in the park. Keeping bears and humans from interacting has helped the population increase. Today, about 700 grizzly bears live there.

Wolves

Like grizzly bears, the number of wolves in the park has also increased. Their howls are a special part of the Yellowstone experience. In 1995 and 1996, 31 gray wolves were relocated from Canada to Yellowstone.

People were not sure whether the wolves would leave the park to eat nearby cattle and sheep. No one knew how the wolves would affect other animal species or the ecosystem in the park.

Now, there are about 100 wolves in Yellowstone. The wolves' presence has helped the park in lots of ways. They have moved elk and deer away from valleys, where they were easy prey for larger animals. Because the elk have moved, trees now grow in those areas. The trees are no longer eaten by the elk.

Wolves hunt and kill coyotes. Fewer coyotes in the park helps animals that are their prey. Foxes also benefit, since they eat the same prey as coyotes. Foxes no longer have to compete for food.

small pack of gray wolves

Wolves howl to signal their pack.

Wonderful Waterfalls

If you like waterfalls, Yellowstone is a great place to visit. The park boasts about 350 waterfalls that are at least 15 ft. (5 m) tall. There are also countless smaller waterfalls called **cascades** in the park.

Two of the most spectacular falls are a short walk from each other. The Upper Falls and the Lower Falls are both on the Yellowstone River. They are easy to get to by road.

The Upper Falls drops 100 ft. (30 m) in a burst of white foam. The Lower Falls drops more than 300 ft. (91 m). Many visitors notice the green stripe in the Lower Falls. This is caused by a lip in the rock behind the water. The lip of a waterfall is the area where the water "bends." The water is deeper in this area. This keeps the water from foaming with the air because of the angle of the lip. This is why the deeper part of the water looks green.

The Grand Canyon of Yellowstone is about 20 mi (32 km) long from the Upper Falls to the Tower Falls area. This narrow canyon is one of the park's most stunning sights. Iron and **sulfur** in the rock give the canyon a rust color. People can hike a trail into the canyon for a close-up view of the falls.

LET'S EXPLORE MATH

In 1871, the U.S. government sent an expedition to Yellowstone. An artist named Thomas Moran created paintings to show Congress why Yellowstone was so special and should be protected.

Imagine that one of his large paintings needs to be restored. It will travel in a 40 cubic meter box to a museum. In the drawings, each cubic unit stands for 1 cubic meter. Which box has a volume of 40 cubic meters?

A.

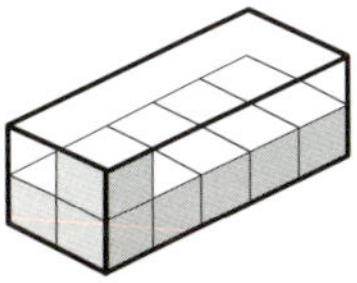

B.

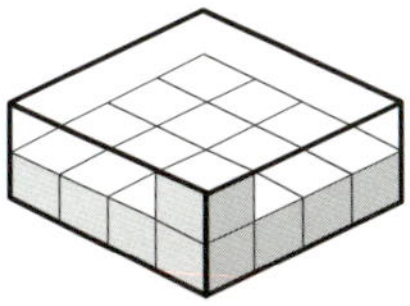

C.

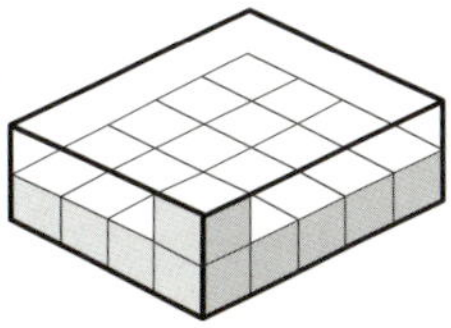

A favorite hiking destination is the remote Cascade Corner. This area gets the most **precipitation** in the park. Its landscape includes lots of steep drops. Those drops create amazing waterfalls!

Terraced Falls is actually a set of six waterfalls in a row. The Falls River descends more than 140 ft. (43 m) to make this waterfall. Terraced Falls is only 2 mi. (3 km) from the road, which makes it an easy trek for hikers.

Union Falls, though, is more than 10 mi. (16 km) away from the nearest road. Yet it is one of the highlights of Cascade Corner. Two streams flow over cliffs right next to each other. This is how the waterfall was named—the two streams come together as one to fall 250 ft. (76 km). This results in a very unique waterfall.

Morning Falls is a 60-ft. (18-m) waterfall in Yellowstone. It is 100 ft. (30 m) wide. As its name suggests, it's best to see it in the morning. It faces the east and sparkles as the early sun rises. People who want to visit this waterfall should beware. The waterfall is not maintained by park staff. Morning Falls is so remote that rangers didn't know about it until 1969!

LET'S EXPLORE MATH

Scientists estimate that during spring, water flows at about 8 cubic meters per second over the waterfalls. Draw three different rectangular prisms that could hold this amount of water. Have each cubic unit in your drawing represent 1 cubic meter.

A Year at Yellowstone

In Yellowstone, snow typically starts to fall in October. Most of the roads are closed by November because of the heavy snowfall. Despite the snowy weather, the park stays open in winter. Many visitors like to see the sights covered in snow. However, visitors might have to ride a snowmobile to see Old Faithful!

Many animals stay hidden during winter. They hibernate or bury themselves in **burrows** under the snow.

Foxes and coyotes stay active during the winter. They must continue to search for food. Predators listen for small animals, such as mice, that hide under the snow. When they hear their prey, it's time to attack! Foxes pounce headfirst into the snow to find their prey. Coyotes dig with their front paws to get their meal.

An American red fox finds a meal.

During winter, wolves follow elk and bison into the valleys to hunt for food. Wolf packs compete for available food.

Bison break into small herds of about 20. They grow thick winter coats that help them stay warm. Bison use their huge heads and strong shoulders to dig through the snow. Other animals often follow behind the bison, using them as snowplows.

This bison's thick fur keeps it warm in the snow.

LET'S EXPLORE MATH

Park roads at Yellowstone close each spring. Clean-up crews use snowplows to remove the winter's snow from the roads. The snow is placed in piles along the sides of the roads.

1. Imagine that one of the snow piles has a length of 9 meters, width of 5 meters, and height of 5 meters. Draw a model of this snow pile. Have each cubic unit in your drawing represent 1 cubic meter.
2. What is the volume of the snow pile?

By spring, Yellowstone is full of life again. In March, adult male bears leave their dens. In April, females emerge with cubs that were born during the winter. The bears feast on **winterkill**. The large animals that died during the winter stay frozen until spring, and they make a perfect meal.

A grizzly bear feeds on winterkill.

Bison calves are born late April into May. After a couple days, they join the herd. Wolf pups are born in April. April is an important month for wolves and bison, too. The wolves and pups abandon their dens by the time the pups are 8 to 10 weeks old.

a wolf and her pups

Soon, the park is crowded with visitors who enjoy the warm summer weather. But, by September, temperatures often drop below freezing. Marmot, a species of ground squirrels, hibernate soon after temperatures dip.

Often, male elk battle over mates. They begin to **rut**, or mate, in October. The males bugle, or make a loud series of noises. This attracts females. It can also be used to warn other males.

The fall season at Yellowstone brings its own changes. In Yellowstone's valleys, the ground cover turns yellow and gives the park a golden hue. Soon, Yellowstone's long winter will return.

An elk bugles during the rut.

Always Enchanting

Yellowstone was made a national park in 1872. The U.S. National Park service helped protect the park. They started to teach people about the wildlife. They raised money to protect the park and to get the public involved. But, more needed to be done. People **poached** animals. They cut down trees. In 1886, the U.S. Army entered Yellowstone to guard it. Park rangers took over in 1918.

The park's borders changed in 1929. The new borders followed natural land features more closely. In 1932, 7,000 more acres were added to the northern border. The changes have not stopped. Plans and laws are revised each year to better protect the park.

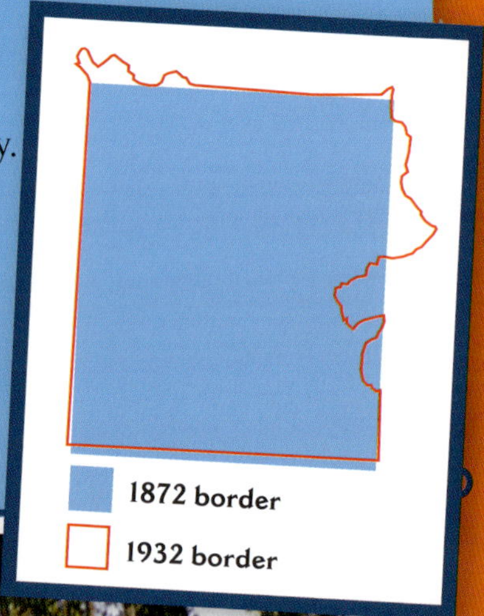

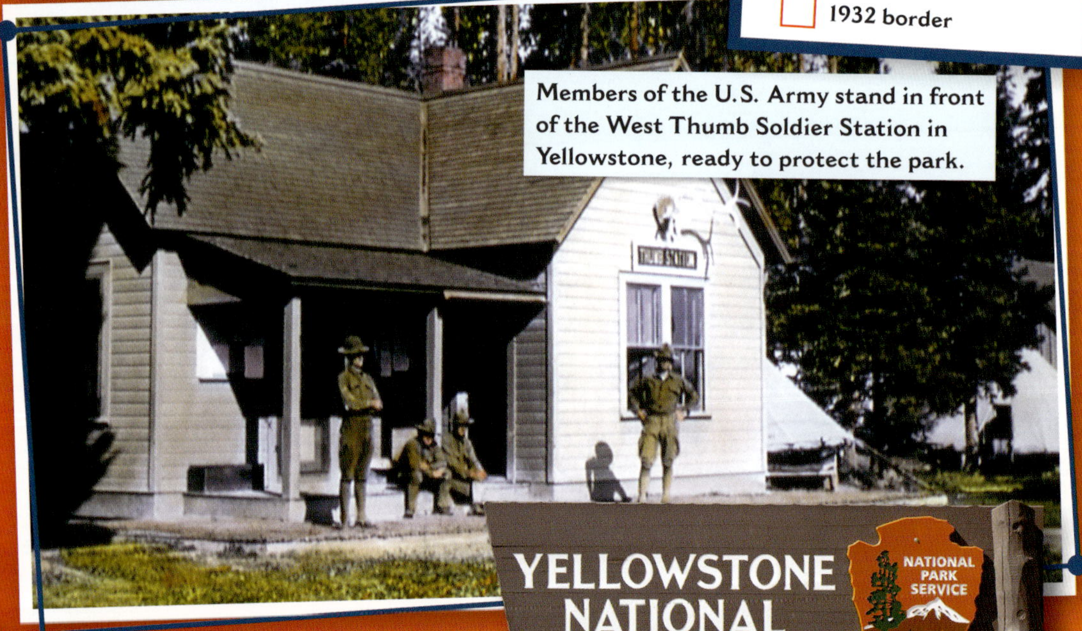

Members of the U.S. Army stand in front of the West Thumb Soldier Station in Yellowstone, ready to protect the park.

A Yellowstone park ranger gets a close look at a giant geyser in the 1880s.

Natural events shape the land and bring changes to Yellowstone. An earthquake in 1998 changed Old Faithful. It made its eruptions longer.

People shape the park, too. More than three million people visit the park each year. Some people at the park cause vandalism, pollution, damage, and overuse.

Most of all, the park changes because it is alive. Wolf packs battle for supremacy. Beaver dams change the flow of streams. It is impossible to count all the ways the park changes! But, one thing that John C. Davis noticed in 1864 remains the same: Yellowstone is an enchanted place!

Problem Solving

Bears have big appetites. Plus, they consider anything with a scent to be food—including garbage! That is why it is important for the dumpsters at Yellowstone to be bear-proof. This is necessary to keep bears and people safe.

Imagine that you are one of the rangers choosing new dumpsters for different areas of the park. Three companies submit different specifications for their dumpsters. All of the dumpsters are shaped like rectangular prisms. Use the details to answer the questions and make the best choices.

1. Calculate the missing specifications for each dumpster.
2. The dumpster with the least volume will be installed at each campsite. Which dumpster do you recommend and why?
3. Picnic areas require dumpsters with twice the volume of the campsite dumpsters. Which dumpster is the best choice for the picnic areas and why?
4. The dumpster behind the visitor's center needs to have the greatest volume.
   a. Which dumpster is best for the visitor's center?
   b. How many times greater is the volume of the dumpster behind the visitor's center than the volume of the campsite dumpster? How do you know?

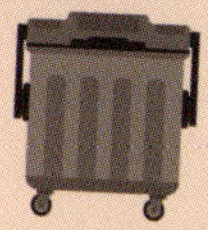

Garbage Solution, Inc.
1243 Boulevard Lane
Dubois, WY 82513
(307) 555-9856

Great Garbage Dumpster
Length: 4 feet
Width: 7 feet
Height: 3 feet
Volume: ________

The Trash Can Man
80915 Avenue Street
Jackson, WY 83002
(307) 555-4857

Bear-B-Gone Dumpster
Length: 6 feet
Width: 7 feet
Height: ________
Volume: 252 cubic feet

Dumpsters-R-Us
4343 Refuse Avenue
Jackson, WY 83002
(307) 555-8383

Tough Trash Dumpster
Length: ________
Width: 7 feet
Height: 4 feet
Volume: 168 cubic feet

Glossary

aggressive—ready and willing to attack, fight, or argue

burrows—tunnels or holes in the ground made by an animal to stay safe or to live in

cascades—waterfalls that are small but steep

contradictions—statements that are different or opposite in meaning

ecosystem—a system of living things and how they interact with their environment

elite—the most successful or powerful group or individual

enchanted—something amazing and delightful

extinct—no longer in existence

magma—hot, melted rock beneath Earth's surface

organisms—living things

plateau—landform that has high elevation and a level surface

poached—illegally hunted or killed

precipitation—any form of moisture that falls from the sky

predators—animals that eat other animals

prospector—someone who searches for gold, minerals, or gems

proximity—closeness

rut—the time when some animals, such as deer, sheep, or camels, seek mates

sulfur—yellow-colored chemical with a strong, foul odor used to make paper, gunpowder, and medicine

thermophiles—tiny organisms that live in extreme heat

winterkill—animals that die in winter and, usually, stay frozen until spring

Index

Answer Key

Let's Explore Math

page 5:

D; Volume is measured in cubic units because there are three dimensions (length, width, height).

page 7:

1. 3
2. 9 cu. cm
3. 27 cu. cm

page 13:

2; 6; 12

page 19:

C

page 21:

Drawings should include rectangular prisms with the following dimensions: 1 × 1 × 8; 2 × 4 × 1; and 2 × 2 × 2.

page 23:

1. Drawings should show a rectangular prism with a 9 × 5 base and a height of 5.
2. 225 cu. m

Problem Solving

1. Volume: 84 cu. ft.; Height: 6 ft.; Length: 6 ft.
2. Great Garbage Dumpster; Its volume of 84 cu. ft. is the least of three dumpsters.
3. Tough Trash Dumpster; Its volume of 168 cu. ft. is equal to 84 × 2.
4. **a.** Bear-B-Gone Dumpster

   b. 3 times; 84 × 3 = 252